SISTERS of the LAST STRAW

The Case of the Stolen Rosaries

But all they saw was Sister Lacey in her bathrobe. She was staring at the empty counter. "Son of a Tiptoeing Thief!" yelled Sister Lacey. "How did they do it?"

"What happened?" asked Mother Mercy, as her face went white.

"The robber got in again! I don't know how he did it! I was sleeping here all night and I didn't hear a thing!"

Also from Chesterton Press

Sisters of the Last Straw
#1 The Case of the Haunted Chapel
#2 The Case of the Vanishing Novice
by Karen Kelly Boyce

For Teens

The Fairy Tale Novels
Fairy tales retold by Regina Doman
www.fairytalenovels.com

The John Paul 2 High Series
by Christian M. Frank
www.johnpaul2high.com

*See all titles and accompanying study
guides at www.chestertonpress.com*

Karen Kelly Boyce

SISTERS
of the
LAST
STRAW

#3 The Case of the
Stolen Rosaries

CHESTERTON PRESS
FRONT ROYAL, VIRGINIA

Dedicated to Heather Tsapp,
My first fan

In memory of my talented friend:
Till we meet again
Karen F. Riley
1962–2013

Text Copyright © 2014 by Karen Kelly Boyce

Cover art copyright © by Sue Anderson Gioulis
Cover and interior illustrations copyright © by Sue Anderson Gioulis
Book design by Regina Doman

Chesterton Press
P.O. Box 949
Front Royal, VA 22630
www.chestertonpress.com

Summary: A renegade rooster terrorizes the Sisters' back yard and a
mysterious thief snatches the Sisters' rosaries in this third advenure
about a convent of misfit nuns.

ISBN: 978-0-9899411-3-6
Printed in the United States of America

Contents

Chapter 1

That Darn Rooster

Sister Krumbles stood looking out the screen door of the kitchen. There was a long staff in her hand. Her hand was shaking. She had to go outside, but she didn't want to. She was afraid.

She was not afraid of robbers. She was not afraid of big dogs. She was not afraid of ghosts. She was afraid of a rooster.

The Sisters in her convent had received the gift of seven chickens and one rooster from a friend, Farmer Murphy. They loved having fresh eggs each morning. It saved the Sisters money to have their own chickens. Sister Krumbles loved the fat hens. But she did not love the rooster. His name was Ronnie. And he was mean.

Sister Krumbles slowly opened the screen door and scanned the yard. She quietly tiptoed outside. Looking around, she didn't see the rooster.

She reached the bin that held the goat food. She opened the metal bin as quietly as she could. She poured the pellets into the feeder as the goats ran from the goat house to get their breakfast.

With the long staff in her hand, Sister Krumbles headed toward the chicken coop. She grabbed a handful of grain and tossed it around for the chickens. "Here Ch…ch…ch…chick!" she whispered. The hens all came running to peck at the grain.

She was almost done with her chores! Sister Krumbles tiptoed toward the kitchen door. Then she heard a loud, "CAW! CAW!" She jumped.

But it was just a large crow. It flew to the old pine tree in the center of the yard.

With a sigh, Sister Krumbles headed for the porch. Just then, Ronnie the Rooster darted out from behind the tree and rushed at her!

"AHHH.....!" screamed Sister Krumbles. The nasty rooster flew toward her, beating his wings. He blocked her way. Taking the staff, she pounded the ground. THUMP THUMP! Startled, the rooster jumped back.

Sister Krumbles took a step back and Ronnie the Rooster took a step toward her. The Sister took another step back and Ronnie moved closer. THUMP...THUMP! went the staff against the ground. Sister Krumbles stepped backward onto the porch. She turned and ran into the kitchen, slamming the door behind her. Ronnie flew right into the door. He cackled in rage.

Sister Krumbles laughed. "Ha! Ha! You didn't get me!" She jumped and waved her arms in a silly dance. "You didn't get me today—yay! You didn't get me today—yay!"

When she stopped, she saw all the other sisters in the kitchen were watching her. Sister Shiny was filling the salt shaker. Mother Mercy and the others were eating breakfast.

Sister Krumble's face turned red. "I was just glad that Ronnie didn't peck me today," she said.

"So we see," said Mother Mercy, the head of the order. "Can't you even feed the animals without causing a ruckus?"

Sister Krumbles hung her head in shame. "I don't know what to do about that rooster! I'm afraid of him!"

Mother Mercy stamped her foot. She had a hard time keeping her temper. "Why did you take all these animals from Farmer Murphy if you are afraid of them?"

"Silly Superior!" said Sister Lacey. "We all should take turns helping with the chickens! After all, we all eat the eggs!"

As soon as she said it, the short sister realized this was not a good thing to say. Sister Lacey always found it hard to watch what she said. She had learned to say funny things instead of bad words. But sometimes she still spoke up when she should be quiet.

She tried again. "Well, we are all afraid of something. Son of a Splashing Swimming Pool! I've been afraid of swimming ever since one of my brothers dunked me in the pool. What are you afraid of, Mother Mercy?"

Mother Mercy thought. As she did, the corners of her frown turned up. She began to smile. "I am afraid of losing my temper!" Everyone laughed.

"I'm also afraid of what would happen if I was not in charge," Mother Mercy said. "I guess that is why I made myself head of the order."

Mother Mercy and Sister Krumbles had started the order of the Sisters of the Last Straw. This order was for sisters who had not been able to stay in other convents because of bad habits. Each of the Sisters in the order had a bad habit that she was trying to overcome. They had to help each other.

"Holy Hilarity!" giggled Sister Lacey. "I guess we are all afraid of something. Jesus would want us to entrust our little fears to Him. He will help us be brave!"

"Yes, but we should still help one another!" said Mother Mercy. "You are right. We will all take turns helping Sister Krumbles feed the animals."

Sister Shiny's eyes opened wide. *I don't want to help Sister Krumbles with her messy projects!* she thought. *Why, the back yard is full of dirt and bugs! Those animals smell! They never take baths! I don't want to get my shoes dirty! I don't want to get my hands dirty!*

The thought of dirt made Sister Shiny dizzy. The room spun around her. She backed away, and tripped over a stool. She tried to grab the counter. Instead she grabbed the big can of salt.

The lid went flying into the air. Salt sprayed everywhere. It covered Sister Shiny! The empty canister landed on Sister Shiny's head. It looked as if she were wearing a tin hat over her veil.

"Poor Sister Shiny!" Sister Krumbles said. "You need a hug!" She reached out her arms. She had dirt on the edge of her habit. She had chicken feathers stuck on her veil. She had a smear of mud on her cheek.

"No!" gasped Sister Shiny. But Sister Krumbles hugged her anyway. Now Sister Shiny was covered with mud, salt, and feathers. She began to shake.

Mother Mercy started to chuckle. "I guess Sister Krumbles is Sister Shiny's biggest fear!"

But then they heard another scream. It was not Sister Shiny. It came from the front of the house. Sister Wanda was screaming. "We've been robbed again!" she yelled.

Sister Wanda was a tall, thin girl. She was a novice in the order. Her chore was to clean the Sisters' gift shop. The Sisters ran the shop to raise money for their good works.

Everyone went out into the hallway. Sister Wanda was running towards them. When she saw the Sisters coming, she stopped. "Screaming Sister Shenanigans! What happened?" asked Sister Lacey.

"The rosaries are gone again!" Sister Wanda said. "I'll show you!" She turned to run back to the shop, but instead she opened the door next to the shop door and dashed inside. There was a thump.

7

"What are you doing in the clothes closet?" Mother Mercy shouted.

Sister Wanda stumbled out of the closet. She was very red. No matter where she was, she always seemed to get lost.

"Please stop running and tell us what happened," Mother Mercy said. "What happened to the rosaries?"

The Sisters' best-selling items were the special rosaries they made of sparkling beads. Last month, the Sisters had discovered several rosaries were missing after a big party. The Sisters thought that someone had come in during the party and taken them. Now they were always very careful to lock the door to the little shop whenever they left.

Sister Wanda said, "Well, yesterday evening, I decided to make some rosaries. I made five pretty rosaries. This morning I put the rosaries here on the counter before we went to pray. After breakfast, I came back to clean the shop. But when I opened the door, all the rosaries I made were gone!"

"Did you forget to lock the door?" Mother Mercy asked.

"I know I locked the gift shop door behind me. I had to unlock it to get back in just now," said Sister Wanda.

Mother Mercy pointed to the window. "Did you leave the window open?"

"I guess I did," said Sister Wanda. "I wanted to air out the shop. But that window is so high off the ground. I did not think that anyone could climb through it."

"Rosary Robbing Rascals!" exclaimed Sister Lacey, "How did the robbers get in?"

Mother Mercy looked around the gift shop in dismay. "I don't know, but I intend to find out! It's time to call the police!"

Chapter 2

Baffling Bandits

Officer Mallon came quickly. The tall officer with dark skin was a good friend to the Sisters. He had helped them solve a mystery before. "What is the problem?" he asked.

"Someone is taking our new rosary beads!" Mother Mercy said. She led him to the gift shop. "All the rosaries on the counter were missing this morning!"

"Have you been locking the door at night?" the policeman asked.

"Oh yes," said Sister Wanda. She told him what happened.

Officer Mallon went outside. He searched the ground outside the gift shop window for footprints.

"Maybe the robbers used a ladder," said Sister Wanda.

Officer Mallon looked closely at the grass. "There are no ladder marks here," he said. "If a robber was using a ladder to climb in the window by day, I think someone would have seen him."

"True," Mother Mercy said. "But the last time someone stole our rosaries, it was also during the day."

Officer Mallon rubbed his chin. "We must have a very smart robber on our hands. We'll have extra units patrol the neighborhood. All of us will watch for the robber."

Everyone felt better. They said goodbye to Officer Mallon and went about their chores.

Sister Lovely took Sister Krumbles aside. She said, "I have an idea for that nasty rooster!"

After their chores were done, the two Sisters went to the back yard. Sister Lovely pulled a big wire cage out of the shed. "That is Gracie's old dog cage!" Sister Krumbles said.

"Gracie is such a big dog now. She would never fit in it!" said Sister Lovely. "Let's clean it out with the hose."

Sister Lovely went to turn on the water. Sister Krumbles began to wash down the cage. She was so busy that she forgot all about the rooster!

Then she heard a loud squawk from behind the shed. "No.....!" she screamed as Ronnie the Rooster flew at her.

Dropping the hose, Sister Krumbles ran to the shed. She slammed the metal door shut. Ronnie the Rooster flew at the door. He pecked and crowed.

Sister Lovely saw everything. She picked up the hose. She aimed it at the rooster and turned it on.

SPLASH! "Kerkoo!" Ronnie crowed. He ran away fast! Soon he was out of sight.

"You can come out now!" Sister Lovely shouted to Sister Krumbles. Sister Krumbles peeked out. Then she came out of the shed. She was dusty and her veil was crooked. "How are we ever going to get him into the cage?" she asked.

The pretty Sister thought. "Get the old pool net from the shed. We can catch him with that!"

Then she saw the rooster. He was peering around the side of the shed. She whispered, "Give me the net. Start to walk away. When he follows you, I will nab him!"

Sister Krumbles was afraid, but agreed. Slowly she walked away while she prayed a Hail Mary. *Please help me be brave*, she thought.

The rooster spread his wings. He ran at Sister Krumbles! Sister Lovely had to run. She lifted the net and swooped it down. The net slammed over Ronnie! He was trapped!

"Hooray!" cheered the Sisters.

Suddenly Ronnie flew up out of the net. There was a large hole in the end. "Oh…!" screamed Sister Krumbles.

But Ronnie didn't want to chase Sister Krumbles anymore. He ran away!

"That was the funniest thing I have ever seen!" someone shouted. The Sisters looked up.

Two children, Anna and Michael, were jumping on an old trampoline and laughing.

The children lived in the small apartment outside the convent chapel. Their parents, Joseph and Mary, had needed jobs, so the Sisters had hired them to clean the house and yard. They were all good friends of the Sisters.

Anna and Michael jumped off the trampoline. "What are you trying to do?"asked Michael.

Sister Krumbles explained, "We are trying to put that nasty rooster in this cage!"

Anna said, "There is a much easier way to get him in the cage!" She and her brother put a bowl of corn deep into the cage. Then everyone hid behind a bush. Soon Ronnie the Rooster came back. He strutted around the yard. He looked at the cage. He saw the food.

He walked straight into the cage and began to eat. He didn't see Sister Lovely as she sneaked up and slammed the cage door shut! Ronnie was trapped at last!

The two Sisters danced in a circle with Michael and Anna. They thanked them and then went inside for lunch.

The table was laid out with very pretty food that Sister Shiny had made. There were salads and sandwiches and tall glasses filled with ice cubes and tea. All the Sisters were delighted. But as they sat to pray, they saw that Mother Mercy was sad.

"What's the matter?" asked Sister Lovely after they had prayed. "Don't you like the lunch?"

Mother Mercy sighed, "The food looks very nice. It's just that with the rosaries being stolen, I don't think we will have enough things to sell this week."

"Bratty Bandits!" said Sister Lacey. "I hope the police capture the robbers! Maybe when they do, we'll get all the stolen rosaries back."

Mother Mercy said, "But if we don't have any rosaries to sell, how are we going to buy food for the poor? I hate to think of people going hungry while we enjoy a beautiful lunch."

The Sisters grew sad. It was true. They had not thought of the poor people who needed the food the Sisters would bring them every week.

Everyone had a hard time eating. Most of the lunch became leftovers. Sister Lacey had never seen the Mother Superior so sad.

"I wish I could do something to cheer her up!" she said to Sister Shiny as they did the dishes.

"I'm afraid only one thing would cheer Mother up: catching the robber who has our rosaries," said Sister Shiny sadly.

That's when Sister Lacey had an idea. *Why wait for the police? I can catch the robber myself!*

That night, Sister Lacey got up. She grabbed her pillow and blanket. She softly stepped down the stairs and the hallway until she reached the gift shop. She went in and locked the door behind her.

The rosaries were locked in a cabinet. Sister Lacey was glad to see they were all there.

She took them out and put them on the counter to count them. *It does not matter if I leave them out,* she thought. *I am here to guard them.*

Then she lay down on the floor to sleep. But it was so hot that she could not sleep. "Son of a Stuffy Stillness!" Sister Lacey whispered. She got up and opened the window to let in some cool night air. Then she lay down again.

But what if the robber comes in the open window? she thought. She had an idea! She moved her blanket and pillow so that she was right under the window. *If anyone comes in the window, they will step right on me and wake me up!* Sister Lacey smiled and yawned. She fell asleep easily, guarding the gift shop.

She dreamed that she captured the robber! The whole neighborhood was grateful. Everyone cheered for her.

Sister Lacey saw herself on large stage in front of thousands of people. The police praised her bravery. Then the Governor put a large golden medal around her neck while everyone cheered.

The President of the United States arrived, landing in a whirling helicopter on the roof. All the people clapped as he congratulated her. He gave her a large bag of money as a reward. It was enough money to buy tons of food. It was enough to feed all the poor in Spring Creek Township for a full year!

With these wonderful dreams in her head, Sister Lacey slept soundly. No noise woke her. No robber stepped on her as she slept under the window. The door did not open. She didn't hear any footsteps. She slept beneath the cool breezes of the open window until the morning light.

When the sun came up, Sister Lacey did not know where she was. Everything was peaceful. Then she remembered that she had slept in the gift shop to catch the robber.

She stood up and stretched. Then she looked at the counter. "Rosary-Robbing Rascals! I don't believe it!" she screamed. All of the rosaries were gone!

Chapter 3

Planning a Surprise

When Sister Lacey screamed, Mother Mercy and all the Sisters came running. Everyone was worried that something bad had happened to Sister Lacey.

But all they saw was Sister Lacey in her bathrobe. She was staring at the empty counter.

"Son of a Thuggish Thief!" yelled Sister Lacey. "How did they do it?"

"What happened? Where are the rosaries?" asked Mother Mercy, as her face went white.

"The robber got in again! I don't know how he did it! I was sleeping here all night and I didn't hear a thing!" said the gray-haired sister.

"Did you lock the door?" asked Sister Shiny

"Oh! Latching Lock! I checked that the door was locked before I fell asleep," said Sister Lacey.

"Was the window open?" asked Sister Wanda.

"Blessed Blowing Breezes....yes! But I slept right beneath the window. If anyone came in they would have stepped right on me!"

"Why were the rosaries on the counter?" asked Mother Mercy.

Sister Lacey was afraid she would make Mother Mercy lose her temper. She did not want to tell her the truth. But she decided to be brave. "I put them there. I thought they would be safe since I was in the room."

Everyone looked at Mother Mercy. They thought she would yell. They thought she would stamp her feet. But she did not say anything. She did not look mad. Instead, she looked sad.

The Sisters were used to Mother Mercy getting mad. They were not used to her being sad.

"We better call Officer Mallon. He'll know what to do!" Sister Krumbles said.

Mother Mercy shook her head. "I am sorry. You are right! We'd better do that."

"I'll do it!" said Sister Wanda, as she ran to the hallway phone. She quickly made the call. But then she forgot where she was. Instead of running back to the gift shop, she ran out the front door.

By the time she realized where she was, the door had shut behind her. The lock clicked.

Sister Wanda pulled on the door handle but it was locked! Sister Wanda was stuck out on the front porch!

Sister Wanda turned red. *Oh no! I don't want the others to know that I made another mistake,* she thought. So she sat in the porch rocking chair. *I will just wait here for the police to come. Then I will go back inside with them,* she decided. She closed her eyes.

After five minutes, someone came up the walk. Thinking it was the police, Sister Wanda rose with a smile.

But the man was not a police officer. It was the Sister's next-door neighbor, Mr. Lemon.

"W—what can I do for you, Mr. Lemon?" Sister Wanda whispered. She did not want to make a scene.

"Get that boss nun out here! I've been robbed and I know it has something to do with you nuns!" the older man yelled.

A police car pulled up to the curb. "Sh…." whispered Sister Wanda. "We've been robbed too, and here are the police. There's no need to shout."

Mr. Lemon said, "I'll shout as loud as I want! There's been nothing but trouble since you nuns moved here!"

Officer Mallon came up just as Mother Mercy opened the door.

"Now, now, Mr. Lemon, you can hardly blame the Sisters for the robberies in the neighborhood! They have been robbed a number of times too." Officer Mallon said.

Mr. Lemon pointed his finger at Mother Mercy. "But they are bringing in all the riff-raff. 'The poor…the poor…!' That's all you hear them talking about. 'Let's help the poor!' Well, the poor are probably the ones who doing the stealing!"

Mother Mercy smiled. "Jesus loved the poor. And He said it was a sin to judge others."

Mr. Lemon's face turned red. "It is also a sin to steal! I am sure once we catch the robber, it will be someone you nuns know!"

Officer Mallon was cross, but he stayed calm. "What did the robbers take from you, Mr. Lemon?"

Mr. Lemon said, "My gold cufflinks! I left them on my nightstand last night. When I got up this morning, they were gone! I looked on the table, the floor, and even under the bed. They've been stolen!"

"I will make a report as soon as I am done here," Officer Mallon said. "Excuse us, Mr. Lemon."

Officer Mallon and all the Sisters went inside. Sister Wanda slipped in with them. She was glad no one noticed that she had locked herself out.

Officer Mallon listened to Sister Lacey's story. "Are you sure the door was locked?" he asked. "And you slept right under the window?"

"Yes and yes! How did they do it?"

"It really is a mystery! We will send out extra patrols tonight. Please make sure that all the doors and windows are locked," he said.

When Officer Mallon had gone, Mother Mercy was very quiet. She walked slowly to her office. She closed her office door with a sigh.

Sister Lovely watched her. When Sister Lovely was sad or worried, she could only think of one thing. Her bad habit was smoking. She had never been able to quit.

After the other Sisters went back to work, Sister Lovely snuck downstairs to the basement. She had hidden a pack of cigarettes there. She wanted to smoke so badly!

She reached for the cigarettes. Then she put them down. She thought of all the trouble she had caused by smoking in the past. She always felt bad after she smoked. She knew Jesus did not like her to sneak and hide.

Sister Lovely sat down on an old metal chair. She began to pray. "Jesus, please help me not to smoke!" She knew she smoked when she was upset. And she was upset to see Mother Mercy so sad. She began to pray for Mother Mercy, too.

Suddenly, she thought of something! Jumping up, she threw the pack of smokes in the trash. She ran up the stairs to find the other Sisters.

Running through the kitchen door, Sister Lovely found the other Sisters having tea at the table. Mother Mercy was not there.

"I've got a great idea!" she said. "Next week is Mother Mercy's birthday! What do you think of giving her a surprise birthday party?"

All the Sisters happily began to plan.

Chapter 4

A Visit to the Farm

The next day, Sister Krumbles went out to feed the animals. Everything was so different! She didn't have to carry a staff to protect herself. She didn't have to look around. She didn't have to listen for the crows of Ronnie the Rooster. She was safe now.

Smiling, she fed the chickens and goats. Then she took a cup of cracked corn to Ronnie's cage. But when she saw Ronnie, she did not know what to think. Ronnie lay in the back of the cage. His feathers were crumpled and dull. He didn't pick up his head to look at Sister Krumbles.

She opened the door just enough to fit the cup of corn and the bowl of water. Quickly she closed the door again. Nothing happened. Ronnie did not come to eat his food or to drink his water. He did not even look up.

Why, he looks sad! Sister Krumbles thought. She felt sorry for the rooster. But she couldn't just set him free. *Maybe I can teach him to be nice,* she thought. *But how?*

Then she knew what to do. *I'll ask Farmer Murphy!* Farmer Murphy had given the Sisters the chickens. Sister Krumbles had never been to his farm. But surely he would know about roosters!

She ran back to the convent. She could not wait to get to the farm.

Mother Mercy gave her permission to go. Soon Sister Krumbles and Sister Wanda were off on the trip. Sister Krumbles was driving and Sister Wanda was holding the map. She told Sister Krumbles which way to go in order to get to the farm.

They left the village on a road that led into a forest. They drove for a long time through woods. First they turned left. Then they turned right. After they turned, the road became a dirt road. Sister Krumbles had to slow down. Dirt and rocks flew in the air.

"We're going to have to wash the car after this trip!" laughed Sister Krumbles.

Sister Wanda was a little scared. This trip was taking too long. *I hope we're not lost!* she thought. She looked at the map again.

Then she saw the map was upside down. She had been telling Sister Krumbles to drive the wrong way!

Sister Krumbles was smiling and humming. She loved road trips. *Poor Sister Krumbles,* thought Sister Wanda, *I hate to tell her that we are lost!*

Sister Wanda was afraid to say something. But then the road dipped down by a river. There was mud and trash all over the road. There was no sign of a farm.

"I can't see the farm anywhere," Sister Krumbles said, "I don't understand what happened."

"I—I think I made a mistake," said Sister Wanda "I think I was holding the map upside down."

Sister Krumbles slammed on the brakes. The brakes screeched as the car came to a stop.

"Are you sure?" asked Sister Krumbles.

Sister Wanda hung her head. "I'm sorry! We are going the wrong way. We have to go back and it is all my fault."

Sister Krumbles was surprised, but then she smiled. "Well! Don't be upset. We all make mistakes! I have made many mistakes and made many messes. No sense in making a fuss!"

Sister Wanda smiled too. "I'm so glad that you're not mad. You make everything so much fun!"

"Let's get out of the car and stretch. We'll take a good look at that map, too," said Sister Krumbles.

The two Sisters got out of the car. They spread the map open on the hood of the car. "Can you see where we are?" Sister Wanda asked.

Sister Krumbles looked and looked. "Ah ha!" she said. She pointed to a small thin road. "Here is where we are!"

Just then, a big wind came and blew the map high into the air!

Sister Wanda jumped to grab the map. But it was too high up. The two sisters ran after the map. It dipped and skipped. Each time it dipped they tried to grab it—but they could not catch it.

Sister Krumbles ran as fast as she could. Her veil was flapping. She put her hands in the air to catch the map. She didn't see the large rock in front of her. Tripping, she fell off the side of the bank.

"Oh..........!" she cried as she skidded down. She landed in the muddy river. Her veil flipped over her face. She pushed it away and looked around. Then she saw the map as it blew into the woods and out of sight. "Oh....no!" she shouted.

Sister Wanda had stopped to help Sister Krumbles out of the river. Sister Krumbles was wet and muddy.

"What can we do now?" she asked.

For a moment Sister Krumbles was sad, but then her face lit up. "We can pray! We can pray to St. Anthony. He is the saint who is good at helping us find lost things!"

Sister Wanda was glad. "Yes! We may not know where the map is, but Jesus knows. I'm sure St. Anthony could ask Jesus to help us."

Sister Krumbles was excited now. "Of course Jesus will help us! Especially when a good friend like St. Anthony asks Him a favor. I always like to help everyone, but I especially like to help people my friends tell me about!"

The two Sisters sat on the river bank and bowed their heads. After making the sign of the cross they both prayed, "St. Anthony, St. Anthony—please come around! Something's lost that can't be found!"

Suddenly, the wind changed. The map flew right toward the Sisters. It flew right into Sister Krumbles' face!

Sister Wanda laughed as she peeled the map off the muddy Sister Krumbles. "Well, that was a quick answer to prayer!"

"Yes! Let's not forget to thank Him! Then we will get back to the car before we lose the map again!" said Sister Krumbles.

Soon the Sisters were back on the road. They headed back the way they had come. After a while, they saw the sign for the farm.

The farm had white fences and a big red barn. When the Sisters drove up, they saw Farmer Murphy. He was putting hay in his truck. He waved at the Sisters.

"Well, hello!" he said. "What brings you to the farm?"

Sister Krumbles told him about Ronnie the Rooster. She said, "I want to make friends with Ronnie so he can be free. I just don't know how."

Farmer Murphy rubbed his chin. "In order to make friends with an animal, you must think as he thinks. God made roosters to protect hens and their eggs. Ronnie thinks that he has to protect his flock. He uses his claws and his beak to peck at strange animals. He runs with his wings out to scare them away. He thinks of you as a strange animal. Why, he's just doing his job!"

Sister Krumbles understood. "I want to help him do his job! But how do I make him know that I am his friend?" she asked

"It is not too hard," said Farmer Murphy. He walked over to the chicken coop. "Watch me!"

Farmer Murphy scattered some grain. As the chickens ran to peck at the ground, he grabbed one of the roosters by both feet.

Upside down, the rooster spread his wings and went limp.

The farmer turned the rooster around. He held him in his arms like a baby. He stroked his feathers. The rooster started to coo. Farmer Murphy fed the bird grain right from his hand. "Now he knows that I mean him no harm. He will come up to me and eat out of my hand without fear."

The Sisters were amazed. "I did not know it would be so easy," Sister Krumbles said. "I am so glad we came!"

"How can we thank you?" Sister Wanda asked.

"I know!" said Sister Krumbles. "You can come to the party we are giving Mother Mercy for her birthday! We would love to have you!"

"I will be happy to come," smiled the farmer.

On the way home, Sister Wanda was careful to hold the map the right way. And Sister Krumbles drove fast. She couldn't wait to get home and make friends with Ronnie.

Chapter 5

Making Friends

Mother Mercy spent a lot of time packing her suitcase. She wanted to be sure she had her toothbrush and a change of habit. She added a Bible and some books she had been trying to find time to read. She sat on the stuffed suitcase. It would not close. She had to bounce up and down to squish the suitcase shut. At last it closed. She was ready.

Each year, the heads of all the convents had to meet with the Bishop. They prayed together and went over their plans for the next year.

Mother Mercy usually hated to leave her friends behind. But this year she was looking forward to it.

I will be glad to have a day or two without worrying about stolen rosaries! she thought.

She carried her suitcase down the stairs. All the nuns gathered in the hallway to wish Mother Mercy a safe trip. Mary the housekeeper and her children were there too.

Mother Mercy gave each Sister a hug goodbye. "While I'm away, Sister Shiny will be in charge. I should be back tomorrow evening or the next morning. And don't forget to pray for me." All the Sisters waved goodbye as Mother Mercy drove away.

"Whew! I thought she'd never leave!" said Sister Shiny.

"Slow-to-Leave Superior!" laughed Sister Lacey. "Now that she's gone, we can plan her party."

"I'll clean the house," said Sister Shiny. She wanted to make the house sparkle.

"I'll go shopping for party treats!" said Sister Wanda. "I can get balloons, hats, and streamers."

"What should we buy her for a present?" asked Sister Lovely.

"Blistering Birthday Bash! I know the perfect present! I'll go buy it!" said Sister Lacey.

"I'll cook all the food," said Sister Lovely.

Michael and Anna wanted to help. "We can make the invitations! We have construction paper and glue!"

Sister Krumbles shouted, "And I'll make her favorite cake—strawberry shortcake!"

The doorbell rang. Mary went to the door. She came back, and said, "Sisters, Officer Mallon and Mr. Lemon are at the front door!"

"And Mother Mercy is not here!" said Sister Wanda. "What shall we do?"

"We must go and talk to them," Sister Shiny said. Everyone followed Mary back to the open front door.

Mr. Lemon stood with a scowl on his face. He looked more mad than ever. Officer Mallon said, "Sisters—were you robbed last night? Mr. Lemon was robbed of a very costly lighter. We were wondering if you heard or saw anything."

Since Mother Mercy was not there, all the Sisters began to talk at once. No one could be understood.

Mr. Lemon shouted, "You see? They know something! They must be covering up for the robber."

"Brother of a Bad-Mouthing Barbarian!"cried Sister Lacey. "We had nothing to do with your stolen lighter!"

"Are you sure you didn't just lose it?" asked Sister Shiny.

"I am sure!" snarled Mr. Lemon. "Last night, I put it on my night stand. When I woke up in the morning, it was gone. I searched the floor and under the bed. It's not lost—it's stolen!"

"Were your windows locked?" asked Sister Krumbles.

"The downstairs windows were locked, but I left my bedroom window open for fresh air," said Mr. Lemon.

"We are sorry that it is missing," said Sister Lovely, "We'll keep our eyes open for it."

Mr. Lemon stomped down the stairs. Before he left, Officer Mallon said, "Please be careful. The robber is still out there."

Back inside the convent, the Sisters went to work. They only had a day to get ready for Mother Mercy's birthday party. They were not about to let Mr. Lemon's complaints stop them.

Sisters Lacey and Wanda went out to catch the bus to go shopping. Sister Shiny began to clean. Sister Lovely and Sister Krumbles went to the kitchen.

Sister Lovely began to make baked ziti. She started by boiling a pot of water for the noodles. She thought Sister Krumbles would start making the cake. But instead, the plump sister put on her coat.

"Aren't you going to start baking the cake?" Sister Lovely asked.

"Oh no! I need the cake to be as fresh as it can be. I will start baking tomorrow," said Sister Krumbles as she went to the door. "Today I am going to make friends with Ronnie the Rooster." Out she went.

Sister Krumbles walked to Ronnie's cage. She was scared, but she felt bad when she saw Ronnie.

He was lying like a lump in his cage. He hadn't touched his food or his water.

Sister Krumbles tried to remember what Farmer Murphy had said to do. "Ronnie—don't be scared! I want to be your friend," she said. Slowly she opened the cage. She grabbed his legs quickly and pulled him out.

Sister Krumbles held the rooster upside down just as Farmer Murphy had done. She was so scared her hand shook. But Ronnie spread his wings and lay limp. So Sister Krumbles walked around the yard holding him upside down.

"Does it feel good to be out of that cage?" she asked. "If you let me be your friend, you can be free again."

Sister Krumbles walked around the yard three times. She prayed and prayed. At last she flipped Ronnie into her arms. She held him like a little baby. But she was still scared he would peck her.

"There," she said. Her legs were shaking. She had to sit down on the back porch.

But she started to pet Ronnie's back. She said in a sweet voice, "You're a nice rooster….What a nice rooster!"

Ronnie didn't move. He did not seem mad. He seemed to like it. Then he began to coo. Sister Krumbles smiled. She and Ronnie were friends!

The afternoon seemed to fly by. When Sister Lovely called her to dinner, Sister Krumbles was surprised. She had spent so many hours with Ronnie the Rooster!

"I'll just put you back in the cage for now," she said. "Just until I'm sure you feel the same about me as I feel about you."

When she put him back, Ronnie stood up in the cage. He pecked at his food and water. He seemed content. "That's a good boy! I'll take you out tomorrow, as soon as I finish baking the birthday cake," Sister Krumbles said. She went inside to see what her Sisters had done.

Sister Lovely had baked pans of ziti and other yummy foods. Sister Shiny had the dining room clean and the silver polished. Sister Wanda and Sister Lacey were home from the store with many bags. They had bought large red strawberries for the cake. Sister Krumbles was thrilled. "They're beautiful!" she exclaimed.

"Let's see the present you brought Mother Mercy!" said Sister Shiny to Sister Lacey.

"Oh…Surprise Spoilers!" the gray-haired sister answered. "You can all be surprised when Mother Mercy unwraps it."

No amount of begging would make Sister Lacey tell what the present was. So each of the Sisters went off to night prayer with different ideas of what it could be.

Sister Shiny remembered that she was in charge so after prayer she walked all through the house. She made sure every door was locked. She made sure each window was shut. She checked the door in the gift shop. It was locked.

All the new rosaries they had made were on top of the counter. They looked so pretty that Sister Shiny did not want to put them back into the cabinet. She made sure the window was locked.

When she looked outside, she saw two policemen. They were sitting in their police car watching the houses. Sister Shiny felt very safe.

She went to bed tired, and dreamed about balloons and birthday cake.

Chapter 6

A Little Powder

Sister Krumbles couldn't wait to spend more time with Ronnie the Rooster. That night she dreamed of him. Ronnie would sit on the porch beside her. He would walk down the sidewalk with her. She even dreamed that he prayed in the chapel with her!

In her dreams, she and Ronnie were best friends. Ronnie could talk just as if he were a person. He wore a hat and a little green vest. He even had a cell phone that he would call her on. He would text her little chicken jokes. One of the jokes was, "Why did the chicken cross the road?" The answer was "Because good-looking Ronnie the Rooster was on the other side!"

Sister Krumbles woke up laughing. Hopping out of bed, she dressed quickly. After she prayed, she went to the kitchen. No one else was up yet. She drank a glass of orange juice. Then she ran out the kitchen door.

Ronnie stood by the door of his cage. He seemed to be waiting for Sister Krumbles. She opened the door and took hold of Ronnie's legs. She quickly turned him upside down. Smiling, she walked around the yard carrying Ronnie. Then she sat on the back porch and cradled him in her arms. Ronnie cooed happily. She thought, *tomorrow I should be able to set him free.*

Sister Krumbles put Ronnie back in his cage. She gave him fresh food and water. He pecked at his food and water. He seemed so happy.

As she went to the house, she heard the crows up in the pine tree calling, "Caw....Caw!" Looking up, she watched the large black crow glide through the air. *Yes,* she thought, *God made birds to fly and be free!*

At the breakfast table, Sister Krumbles couldn't help grinning.

"Are you going to start making the birthday cake after morning prayers?" asked Sister Lovely. "I finished making all the food, so the kitchen is all yours today."

"Nope!" answered Sister Krumbles. "There's plenty of time! I'm going to spend the day with Ronnie the Rooster! I'll make the cake tonight!"

Sister Shiny was upset. "I plan on cleaning the kitchen top to bottom after lunch today. I don't want you making a mess after that!"

"Oh, don't worry! I will clean up myself. I don't want to make the whipped cream topping too early. It's best fresh!" said Sister Krumbles.

The others were dismayed. But no one wanted to hurt Sister Krumbles' feelings.

On the way to the chapel, Sister Shiny checked the gift shop. The door was locked. All the rosaries were still on the counter. "I wonder if the police have caught the thieves," she said.

"Oh Crime-Solving Cops!" laughed Sister Lacey. "I hope so!"

Sister Lovely was worried. Everything was ready for the party. The children had sent beautiful invitations to the Sisters' neighbors and friends. Thanks to Sister Shiny, the house was clean and neat. Sister Wanda had made signs and blown up all the balloons. All of the food was cooked. Everything was ready—everything except the birthday cake.

Sister Lovely watched Sister Krumbles play outside with the animals all day. She seemed to have forgotten about the cake. Sister Lovely did not want to chide her. But at suppertime, the cake was not made. Sister Lovely thought that something should be said.

"Sister Krumbles, what about the cake?" she asked.

"Holy Cooking Catastrophe! Didn't you bake the cake yet?" asked Sister Lacey.

"Oh, don't worry! I will bake the cake tonight after evening prayers. It should only take an hour or two!" Sister Krumbles said.

"But Mother Mercy said that she might actually get home tonight!" said Sister Wanda.

"Even if she gets home tonight, I will be able to make the cake!" laughed Sister Krumbles. "I can be quiet as a mouse! I can be as fast as a bee!"

The Sisters just shook their heads. But they were happy to see Sister Krumbles go to the kitchen after evening prayers.

"Thank God Mother Mercy hasn't come home yet!" Sister Lovely said.

"Well, I will get up early tomorrow! I've seen the kitchen after Sister Krumbles bakes!" said Sister Shiny. All the Sisters giggled as they headed to bed.

Sister Krumbles looked for a cake pan. The kitchen had many round cake pans in all different sizes. Then Sister Krumbles had an idea! She could bake many cakes of different sizes. Then she could stack them to make a very, very tall cake!

I will have to triple the batter to make enough cake, she thought. *I will have to use three times as much of everything.*

Grabbing the butter, she knocked some milk over on the floor. *I'll clean that up later,* she thought. She put the butter in the mixer bowl.

Now she thought *I have to use three times the amount of sugar!* She reached up to get the can of sugar. As she did, she knocked down the can of coffee. Coffee spilled all over the stove and floor. *I'll sweep that up later!* she thought. She added the sugar to the butter.

Now she needed to add three times the amount of eggs. She took two cartons of eggs from the fridge. She slipped on the spilled milk and dropped one of the cartons! The eggs hit the floor and cracked. The yolks ran down the cracks in the tile floor. *Well, one dozen eggs are enough. I'll wash the floor when I'm done!*

"Buzz…zzz!" whirled the mixer. Sister Krumbles tripled the amount of salt. She only spilled a little. Then she went to add the flour. "One….two…. three…four…cups!" she counted as she poured.

Oh no! I will need twelve cups of flour, not just four! There was no more flour left! Sister Krumbles looked but she couldn't find any more flour. *I will just have to see how it comes out,* she thought. As she moved things on the shelf, she knocked over a box of bread crumbs. Crumbs scattered all over the counter and the floor. *I'll sweep them up after the cake is in the oven!* she decided.

She stirred the batter. Sister Krumbles hoped it would make a thick, rich batter. But the mix was like white water. The mixer splashed it everywhere.

Now what? she thought. *I have to thicken it!* She searched for a while, but she could not find any flour.

But she did find baking powder. The baking powder was white. It looked like flour. It tasted a little like flour. She added some to the batter. It thickened a little. There were four cans of baking powder on the shelf. *It can't hurt to use more.*

"One can....two cans...three cans....four! Just keep adding more, more, more!" she sang.

She added six full cans of the baking powder. Now the batter was perfect: thick and rich! *I just have to grease the pans.*

But now she began to yawn. She thought, *I will just make one big cake after all.* She greased the largest pan. She poured all the batter into it. Then she put the pan into the oven. *I need to clean up the kitchen,* she thought. But now she was very tired. *I will just sit down for a while.* When she sat down, she could hardly keep her eyes open. *I will just put my head down and rest.*

She put her head down on the kitchen table. Before she knew it, Sister Krumbles was asleep.

Sister Shiny woke up with a start. She heard a strange noise downstairs. *Is it the robber?* When she sat up, she saw it was still dark. There was a strange smell in the air. Then she heard the noise again.

"Waaah....aaah...zzzh...bang!"

Sister Shiny jumped out of bed and put on her robe. *What is Sister Krumbles doing down there?*

Then she heard the sound again: "WAAAH… AAAH…ZZZH…CLANG!"

She ran into the hallway. The other Sisters were looking out of their rooms. "What is that?" shouted Sister Lovely. "It sounds like the oven!"

All of the Sisters ran downstairs. They ran so fast. They didn't even see Mother Mercy coming through the front door.

In the kitchen, the oven door was open. It looked as if a giant balloon was growing inside.

"It's Sister Krumble's cake!" yelled Sister Wanda.

Sister Krumbles woke up with a jump. When she saw the huge cake, her mouth dropped open.

"Creepy Cake Calamity!" yelled Sister Lacey. "Get out of the kitchen, Sister Krumbles!"

Sister Krumbles ran to stand with the rest of the Sisters. With big wide eyes she watched the strange cake!

The balloon continued to grow! It was as big as the stove. "WAAAH…WAAAH...ZZZZ!" it hissed as it grew larger and larger.

Suddenly the hissing grew louder. With the hissing "ZZZ!" the balloon deflated. As the cake shrunk, the Sisters moved toward it. Then the cake started to grow again. The crowd of Sisters stepped back in fear. In and out the batter balloon went. Back and forth the Sisters went. The cake seemed to be breathing. With each breath it grew larger. "WAAAH!...WAAAAH!...ZZZZ!" The noise grew louder and louder as the batter grew!

"Oh Bursting Batter Blobs!" shouted Sister Lacey as she realized what was about to happen.

"Duck!" shouted Sister Shiny as the blob expanded. The Sisters all fell to the floor.

The cake blob exploded! It blew thousands of bits of hot batter all over the kitchen! Bits of batter hit the cabinets. Bits of batter hit the walls. Bits of the batter hit the Sisters.

The Sisters got to their feet. "I am sorry!" whispered Sister Krumbles.

"What on earth did you put into that cake?" asked Sister Lacey.

"I ran out of flour, so I used baking powder instead," said Sister Krumbles.

"Oh, Careless Cookery!" shouted Sister Lacey. "Don't you know that too much baking powder explodes?"

"I thought it would make the batter thick!" said Sister Krumbles.

Sister Lovely was upset. "If you had baked the cake when I was here," she said, "I would have told you. If you had baked instead of playing with the animals all day, this would not have happened!"

Sister Krumbles knew that Sister Lovely was right. She should have made the cake sooner. She was about to say this, when she saw something else even more terrible than a cake batter bomb.

Mother Mercy was standing in the kitchen doorway. She was covered with cake batter. Her face was so red that she looked like a human bomb about to explode.

Chapter 7

A Shining Example

The other Sisters turned around. They saw Mother Mercy. No one knew what to say.

There were broken eggs all over the floor with bread crumbs soaking in the yolk. There was ground coffee all over the stove and counter with watery batter mixed in. Dried milk was spilled on the floor in front of the fridge. And there were bits of batter everywhere.

Mother Mercy wiped the cake batter from her red face. And she exploded with loud words.

"WHAT IS THE MATTER WITH YOU?" shouted Mother Mercy at Sister Krumbles. "Why were you outside playing with the animals all day instead of doing your work?"

She waved her arms in the air. "AND WHAT IN THE WORLD WERE YOU DOING, BAKING A CAKE IN THE MIDDLE OF THE NIGHT?"

The other Sisters did not know what to say. How could they defend Sister Krumbles without ruining the surprise?

At last, Sister Lovely said, "She didn't mean to make a mess!"

"AUGH!" answered Mother Mercy. "She never MEANS to make a mess, but she always does—doesn't she?"

"I will clean it all up myself," Sister Krumbles said.

"NO! Stay out of trouble and go outside with the animals!" yelled Mother Mercy. "And STAY outside with the animals!"

Sadly Sister Krumbles went out the kitchen door. The sun was coming up outside.

Mother Mercy's face was still red with anger. She went to the sink and got a rag. She began to clean up the floor. The other Sisters ran to help her.

No one said anything. No one knew what to say. They waited for Mother Mercy to calm down.

But Mother Mercy's temper didn't get any better. She kept growling about Sister Krumbles. "Why is she always so careless and messy?"

Sister Lovely started to wonder if there was more to it. "How did your meeting with the Bishop go?" she asked.

Mother Mercy's face turned from red to white. She sighed, "Mr. Lemon has been calling the Bishop every day. Mr. Lemon seems to think that we caused the robberies by caring for the poor and bringing the needy into the neighborhood."

"Oh Lousy Laments!" said Sister Lacey, as she finished mopping the floor. "Does that man do nothing else but complain?"

"If we can't solve the mystery of who is taking the rosaries, we may have to leave this convent. The Bishop may transfer us to another town!" said Mother Mercy.

No wonder Mother Mercy was so upset!

Sometimes when we are upset about one thing, we get angry about another thing, thought Sister Lovely as she finished wiping the counters. *We take out our feelings on someone else. That is why she lost her temper with Sister Krumbles.*

Trying to make things better, Sister Lovely asked, "Can Sister Krumbles come back inside?"

Mother Mercy squared her shoulders. "No! Let her think about what she did." She walked into her office and slammed the door.

Sitting outside, Sister Krumbles told the goats how sad she was. They nodded their heads as she spoke. Sister Krumbles petted their soft ears. She tickled their chins. She wished that she had listened to Sister Lovely. *If I had made the cake sooner none of this would have happened.*

Sadly, she visited the chickens. There were some new eggs in the nests. She wondered if they would have any new baby chicks soon.

She thought of how she had spent all yesterday playing outside when she should have worked. Now she could not go back inside and help her sisters, even though she wanted to. *I did everything backwards!* she thought.

Sister Krumbles decided to take Ronnie the Rooster out of his cage. She held him upside down. Then she walked him around the yard to calm him. *I wonder if this would work with Mother Mercy?* she thought. She smiled at the idea of holding Mother Mercy upside down.

After a while, Sister Krumbles went to sit on the back porch. But then she thought of how upset Sister Lovely had been. She thought of what Sister Lacey had said, and how Sister Shiny had screamed. It was not just Mother Mercy who was upset with her. It seemed everyone was.

So Sister Krumbles walked away from the kitchen. She went to the pine tree and sat down.

As she stroked Ronnie, she told him her troubles. "It's so easy to talk to you," she whispered.

She sighed. "You can always tell animals your troubles, and they never yell at you. I think God made animals to be our special friends."

Sister Krumbles leaned her head back against the pine tree. She looked up to the sky to pray for help. Something shiny almost blinded her. Something at the very top of the tree sparkled in the sun. *What is that?* she wondered.

The more she looked, the more colors she saw: red, blue, green, and purple sparkled in the branches. She decided to climb up the tree. *I will find out what's up there!* she thought.

She put Ronnie the Rooster down. It was very hard to reach the first branch. But she did! She grabbed the branch with both hands. She could not get up higher.

I have to get my feet up on the branch, she thought. She swung her legs back and forth. Pine needles fell down onto her face. She swung her body harder and harder until she swung up and over the branch!

"Whoa....ooa!" she yelled as she almost lost her grip. She stood up and climbed up to the next branch, and the next. Soon she was so high in the tree that she could not see the ground.

"Baa.....aaa!" all the goats cried as they looked up at Sister Krumbles.

"Cluck....uck!" said the hens.

However, the loudest of all the animals was Ronnie the Rooster. "Doo......dle.....do!" he cried. He ran around and around the yard, crowing.

Anna and Michael came outside to see what all the commotion was. They looked up in the tree. They watched Sister Krumbles grab a branch with both hands. It snapped and she began to fall!

"Ah....ah!" she cried. But she grabbed another branch and clung to it.

"We better get help!" shouted Michael. They ran to the convent to get the other Sisters. All the Sisters ran into the yard. When they looked up, they saw Sister Krumbles in the tree! "Come down!" they all yelled.

Sister Krumbles was scared when she looked down. Then she looked up. She saw the shining object was only ten feet away. *I'm not going to give up now!* she thought.

It shimmered with so many different colors. Sister Krumbles couldn't even guess what it could be. She tried to reach the next branch above her. It was a little too far away. *I'll just have to make a jump for it,* she thought. Up she jumped!

But she could only grab it with one hand! "Sister Krumbles!" Mother Mercy screamed.

Sister Krumbles was hanging by one hand. Her veil flapped in the wind. As they watched, she lifted her arm. She grabbed the branch with both hands. She pulled herself up.

"Sister of a Squirrel!" shouted Sister Lacey.

"Get the trampoline under her!" said the quick-thinking Sister Lovely.

The Sisters grabbed the rim of the round trampoline and pulled it under Sister Krumbles. "Come down! Come down!" they shouted to her.

But she did not seem to hear them. Hand over hand Sister Krumbles climbed. The branches were thinner at the top. The tree began to sway.

But the prize was close at hand. She stretched out her hand to the shining mass. It was sitting in a tangle of thorny branches.

The Sisters all moaned, "Oh…..oooooo!" as Sister Krumbles swayed to the right.

The Sisters squealed, "Ah…..aaaaa!" as the top of the pine tree bent to the left.

But Sister Krumbles reached for the thing again. She snatched it from the tree. The branch broke. She fell!

Through the tree's branches she fell! Her veil caught on twigs. Her habit caught on the branches. The Sisters moved the trampoline beneath her as fast as they could.

Sister Krumbles landed straight onto it, with the shiny prize in her hands! Up and down she bounced! At last she lay still, covered with twigs and needles.

Her face was red and scratched. But in her hands was a big shiny thing. It was made of twigs and pine needles. Woven through it were strings of beads and golden things.

It was a crow's nest! And it was made out of rosary beads! Right in the middle were two golden cufflinks and a silver lighter.

Two crows flew in the air over the tree. "Caw! Caw!" they said. They sounded very mad.

"Are you okay? Did you break any bones?" asked Mother Mercy.

"I'm fine," said Sister Krumbles. She sat up and Mother Mercy hugged her tightly. Sister Lovely smiled and thought, *Mother Mercy does love Sister Krumbles.*

"Oh, Crowing Criminals! I think we found our thieves!" shouted Sister Lacey.

"We'd better make sure," said Sister Lovely. "Let's do a test."

All the Sisters followed Sister Lovely as she went to the gift shop.

She took some unfinished rosaries out of the Sisters' work baskets. She put them on top of the counter. Then she made sure that the window was wide open.

All of the Sisters hid behind the door and watched. Within a few minutes, one of the crows landed on the windowsill. It looked around, then flew right to the counter. It scooped up a string of beads in his beak, and flew straight out the window!

"Who would have thought that a bird could be a robber!" giggled Sister Krumbles.

"Flying Felons!" laughed Mother Mercy, sounding like Sister Lacey. "Wait till we tell the Bishop! I'll call him right away."

She smiled. All of the other Sisters smiled too. It was so good to see Mother Mercy happy again.

Chapter 8

A Big Party

"ZZZZ......SHHHHH!" came the snores from Mother Mercy's room. Past the sleeping Superior's room and down the stairs the Sisters tiptoed.

No one spoke as they snuck down the hall. They reached the kitchen. Then they turned on the lights and set to work. It was time to make the cake!

Sister Lacey sifted the flour. Sister Lovely beat the eggs. Sister Wanda creamed the butter. Sister Krumbles greased the pans. Sister Shiny stood like a guard with a wet dishrag in her hand.

She followed everyone, especially Sister Krumbles. She wiped up each tiny drop or spill as they worked. She cleaned every spoon and bowl. Soon the cake was in the oven.

73

Looking around, all the Sisters were amazed. "Oh Spotlessly Shiny!" whispered Sister Lacey. "No one would guess that we just made a cake!"

"Good job, Sister Shiny!" Sister Krumbles said. "We could not have done it without you!"

"The cake should be done by the end of morning prayers," said Sister Wanda. "I'll take it out to cool once Mother Mercy goes to her office. While she is busy there, we can decorate the cake and the house."

After prayer, the yummy smell of baking cake filled the convent. The other Sisters wondered if Mother Mercy would smell it. But she seemed too happy to notice after her phone call to the bishop. She was so happy that the mystery of the stolen beads had been solved.

Once Mother Mercy shut her office door, her Sisters went to work. Sister Wanda tied balloons to all the chairs. Sister Shiny hung the streamers and the signs. Sister Krumbles decorated the cake with whipped cream and strawberries.

Sister Lacey put out all the plates and glasses. Sister Lovely heated all the trays of food.

The guests began to arrive. Michael and Anna stood on the porch to let them in so that the doorbell would not ring. At last, everything was ready. Sister Lovely knocked on Mother Mercy's door.

"Mother Mercy!" she asked. "Could you come to the kitchen and help me with something?"

Mother Mercy came out of the office with a smile. When she reached the kitchen door, Sister Lovely stood back. She let Mother Mercy open it.

Everyone jumped out. "Surprise!" the guests yelled, "Happy Birthday!"

Mother Mercy was stunned! She had forgotten all about her birthday. She was so happy that she grinned from ear to ear. One by one, all the guests kissed her cheek. They each wished her another year of joy. Sister Krumbles led her into the dining room.

There, the very tall strawberry shortcake stood.

It glowed with many candles. Everyone sang "Happy Birthday!"

"My favorite kind of cake!" Mother Mercy cried. Sister Krumbles cut her a large slice of the freshly baked cake.

Suddenly, Mother Mercy's face grew red. But she was not mad. She was very sad. "This is why you were baking that cake in the middle of the night, wasn't it?" she asked Sister Krumbles. "Oh no! I can't believe I yelled at you when you were baking a birthday cake for me!" Mother Mercy put her head into her hands and began to cry. "When will I learn to control my temper?"

Sister Krumbles went to her friend Mother Mercy and hugged her tight. "Jesus is helping all of us. He'll give us the grace to change if we ask Him," she said.

Mother Mercy hugged her back. "Can you ever forgive me?"

Sister Krumbles hugged her back. "I will always forgive you!" All the Sisters smiled.

"Now's the perfect time for you to open your birthday present!" announced Sister Lacey. She set the present in front of Mother Mercy.

Excited, Mother Mercy tore at the bow and the papers. Inside was a large sign with a long prayer on it. There was a border of flowers of many colors around the words. "Why, it's beautiful!"

"'The Prayer of St. Francis,'" Sister Lovely read the words at the top. "Please read it to us, Mother Mercy," said Sister Lovely.

Mother Mercy read:

LORD, make me an instrument of Your peace.

Where there is hatred, let me sow love,

Where there is injury, pardon,

Where there is doubt, faith,

Where there is despair, hope,

Where there is darkness, light,
Where there is sadness, joy.
O divine Master,
grant that I may seek not so
much to be consoled as to console,
To be understood as to understand,
To be loved as to love,
For it is in giving that we receive,
in pardoning that we are pardoned,
And in dying to self that we are born
to eternal life.

All the Sisters and their guests were moved. Mother Mercy wiped away a tear. "I'm going to put this in my office so I can read it every day," she said.

"I will hang it for you!" said Sister Krumbles. And she ran out of the room.

Everyone was enjoying the cake and other food when the doorbell rang.

In came the Bishop and Mr. Lemon! Everyone was surprised!

"What brings you here?" asked Mother Mercy.

"I wanted to wish you a happy birthday, Mother Mercy," said the Bishop. "I brought your neighbor along because I want him to be here when Officer Mallon comes over. He should be here any minute."

The Bishop walked around, shaking hands and blessing people. But Mr. Lemon would not smile at anyone. He would not take the piece of cake Sister Shiny offered him.

Officer Mallon arrived. The policeman had a big grin on his face. He wished Mother Mercy a very happy birthday.

"Well, Bishop," said Mr. Lemon, "you promised if I came with you to this stupid party, you would tell me who the robber is. Who is it?"

The Bishop grinned and said, "The robbers live right next door to you!"

"What?" yelped Mr. Lemon, "So you're saying that the Sisters are the robbers?"

"By no means," said the Bishop. "But robbers are your neighbors!" He led Mr. Lemon to the window. "Look up the old pine tree. The robbers live there!"

Mr. Lemon looked out the window. "Are they so poor that they are living in a tree house?" He looked as though he thought he would see some poor people living in a tree.

"Not a tree house, a nest!" said the Bishop. "The robbers are those two crows. They live in the pine tree between your house and the convent."

"Crows?" yelled Mr. Lemon. "Why would a crow steal?"

"Crows and ravens build nests out of shiny objects," said Farmer Murphy. "They hunt all around and they steal whatever they find. But of course they do not know that they are stealing."

"Here is the proof!" said Officer Mallon. He showed him the large crows' nest made of rosaries. "Here are your cufflinks and lighter. They were part of this nest high up in the tree! The Sisters found them there!"

Mr. Lemon did not say thank you. He took his things and stomped out of the house. "I don't believe it! A bird!...a bird!" he growled.

After he was gone, Mother Mercy said sadly, "He can't believe it wasn't us. He wants to believe that we caused all the trouble."

The Bishop smiled. "I guess the truth 'flies' in the face of what he wants to believe." Everyone laughed. The Bishop joined the party and the merriment continued.

Sister Krumbles was too busy to enjoy the fun. She wanted to hang St. Francis's Prayer perfectly on Mother Mercy's wall. Looking around, she saw the cross high over the desk. *That is the perfect place! Every time Mother Mercy looks up at Jesus, she will see the prayer!*

But the spot was too high to reach. Then she remembered there was a ladder in the shed out back. She hurried to get it.

Sister Krumbles was very careful as she carried the ladder into the office. She was careful when she set up the ladder. It unlocked with a latch. She was careful as she laid it against the wall. She was extra careful as she climbed up the ladder with the hammer, nails, and sign.

"Bang!—bang!—bang!" It only took three hits to get the nail just right. Sister Krumbles hung the prayer. It was perfect. *That went very well,* she thought. She grabbed the ladder but she did not close the latch.

Then she heard a man laughing. *That sounds like our bishop!* she thought. *Is it really him?*

She just had to go and peek in the dining room. When she saw the bishop, she was stunned and ran to greet him. She forgot she was holding the ladder. The end of the ladder came unlatched and swung out. Everyone ducked so that they would not get hit.

"Sister Krumbles, be careful!" Sister Wanda cried.

"Of what?" asked Sister Krumbles. She turned around to see Sister Wanda. The end of the ladder flew around the other way. The Bishop ducked. Mother Mercy ducked. All the guests ducked. But the strawberry shortcake could not duck.

The ladder hit the top layer of the cake. The creamy shortcake flew through the air. It flew right out the window!

There was an angry shout outside. Everyone ran to look. The cake had hit Mr. Lemon in the face. He had been standing next to the pine tree with a rock in his hand. Maybe he was going to throw it at the crows. But now he had whipped cream on his face. Two strawberries slid down his face over his eyes.

He wiped off his face. Then he yelled, "You nuns are nothing but trouble! I will fix you!" He started to throw the rock at the Sisters as they looked out the window.

But just then there was a "Kerkoo Kerkoo!" And Ronnie the Rooster rushed over. His wings were spread. He pecked Mr. Lemon's legs hard.

Mr. Lemon yelled. He dropped the rock and ran. He did not stop running until he was back inside his house.

Ronnie the Rooster stopped at the edge of the Sisters' yard. He fluffed his tail. He strutted back and forth. "Roosters protect what belongs to them," Farmer Murphy said. He winked at Sister Krumbles.

Sister Krumbles was so proud of Ronnie that she wanted to give him a hug. After she brought the ladder back to the shed, she did just that.

When the last guest had left, the Sisters cleaned up from the party. "I'll sleep well tonight," said Sister Lovely.

"Oh! Before we go to pray, I have something for you," said Mother Mercy, "There is a letter you will want to see." She took it out of her pocket and unfolded it. "Your cousin wants to come and visit. over Thanksgiving week. Isn't that wonderful?"

Sister Lovely smiled. "Yes, it is. But I have so many cousins. Which cousin is it?"

Mother Mercy looked back down at the letter. "Her name is Miss Gabby Fibber, and she says she should arrive by train."

Looking up, Mother Mercy saw all the color drain from the pretty Sister's face. Mother Mercy was stunned. *Why is she so afraid?* wondered the Mother Superior.

**Please join
the Sisters of the Last Straw in
their next adventure:**
The Case of the Thanksgiving Visitor!

About the Author
Karen Kelly Boyce

Karen Kelly Boyce lives on a farm in New Jersey with her husband, Michael. She is a member of the Jackson Writer's Group, The Catholic Writer's Guild, and the Central New Jersey Catholic Writer's Guild. With two grown children, Amanda and Michael, she and her retired husband like to travel and enjoy road trips across the country.

Karen is best known for her adult series of novels which are based on the graces of the Rosary. Her three published novels are *According to thy Word, Into the Way of Peace,* and *Down Right Good.* All three have received the Seal of Approval from the Catholic Writer's Guild, and *Down Right Good* has won the Eric Hoffer Award for commercial fiction.

She has also published one non-fiction work on her experience with cancer. *A Bend in the Road* teaches cancer patients how to become cancer survivors with humor, understanding, and practical advice. All the proceeds from this book go to the research department of The Cancer Institute of New Jersey.

With the birth of her two grandchildren, Conner and Kaitlyn, Karen started a series of children's books called the *Sisters of the Last Straw.* This is the third book of the series.

All of Karen's books can be found online on her website, **www.queenofangelsfarm.com.**

About the Illustrator
Sue Anderson Gioulis

Sue Anderson Gioulis completed her art training at Ringling College of Art and Design in Sarasota, Florida.

She is the illustrator of the children's books *Off We Go* and *You're Lovable to Me*, and her drawings and graphic designs are displayed in several states on the East Coast.

Sue is a member of the Manasquan River Group of Artists in New Jersey. She enjoys life by the shore with her family in Ocean Grove, New Jersey. Her work can be viewed online at: **www.gioulisgraphics.com.**

CHESTERTON PRESS
publishes fun Catholic fiction that evangelizes the imagination by telling a good story, inspired by the innocent wit and wisdom of the great English writer G. K. Chesterton. You can find us online at www.chestertonpress.com.